Winnie AND Wilbur

WINNIE
the Bold

The Little Ordinaries

Tiger

Jerry

For Vangelis and Panayiotis, two happy little boys who
make a noise outside my studio window—K.P.
For everyone at Bishop Wood Junior School in Tring—xx

OXFORD
UNIVERSITY PRESS

Great Clarendon Street, Oxford OX2 6DP

Oxford University Press is a department of the University of Oxford.
It furthers the University's objective of excellence in research, scholarship,
and education by publishing worldwide. Oxford is a registered trade mark of
Oxford University Press in the UK and in certain other countries

First published in 2015
This edition first published in 2016

British Library Cataloguing in Publication Data
Data available

ISBN: 978-0-19-274848-5 (paperback)

2 4 6 8 10 9 7 5 3 1

Printed in Great Britain

Paper used in the production of this book is a natural,
recyclable product made from wood grown in sustainable forests.
The manufacturing process conforms to the environmental
regulations of the country of origin.

LAURA OWEN & KORKY PAUL

Winnie AND Wilbur

WINNIE
the Bold

OXFORD
UNIVERSITY PRESS

CONTENTS

WINNIE'S
Hat Trick

53

WINNIE
the Bold

75

WINNIE'S
New Kitten

'Hey, Wilbur, catch this!' said Winnie,
tossing a pongberry towards him. But
Wilbur didn't leap up and catch the berry
in his mouth. He didn't bat the berry back
to Winnie. In fact he didn't even open an
eye or twitch a whisker, as the pongberry
bounced off his head—**ping!**

Snore, he went. **SNORE!**

'You're no fun these days!' said Winnie.
Then she tickled Wilbur behind his left
ear, and she put on a sweety-tweety voice.

7

'Play with me, Wilbur. Pleeease little-tadpole-sneeze? I'll cook you fish fingers and fish toes too if you do.' But Wilbur just carried on snoring.

Winnie sighed. 'When you were a kitten, you played all the time. You were as fun as a bun on the run! Now you're old and fat and boring...'

SNORE!

'. . . so I think I'll get myself a new kitten!' said Winnie.

Suddenly Wilbur *was* awake.

'Mrrrrow!' he said, meaning, 'I thought you loved me!'

But Winnie had made up her mind.

'The new kitten won't be *instead* of you,' Winnie told him. 'It will be *as well as* you. After all, we've got lots of room.'

'Meeow!' protested Wilbur again. But
Winnie took her wand from her pocket,
and was opening her mouth to make magic
when . . .

Ding-dong-smelly-pong! went
the dooryell.

'Whoever . . . ?' said Winnie, pulling open
the door.

There, on her doorstep, was a man in a cap. He was holding a tablet and there was a big box beside him.

'Erm, I'm not exactly sure I'm in the right place,' said the man, scratching his head. 'You don't look like a zoo keeper. Erm, are you expecting a delivery of a feline kind?'

'I don't know,' said Winnie. 'What is a "feline kind"?'

'"Feline" means "cat",' said the delivery man. 'I have a young feline in this box here.'

'Oh, that's perfect!' said Winnie, clasping her hands together. 'Purr-fect, in fact! However did you know . . . ?'

'Just sign here,' said the man, looking pointedly at his watch, and tapping his foot.

So Winnie squiggled a signature.

Then she heaved the box inside, and shut the door.

'Well!' she said. 'Do you want to open it, Wilbur, or shall I?'

Wilbur crossed his arms and scowled. So Winnie lifted the flaps, and . . . out

13

leapt a big beautiful stripy young cat!

'Ooo, look, Wilbur!' said Winnie. 'He goes with my tights! Isn't he handsome?'

Hisss! went Wilbur.

'Now don't be as mean as a cross baked bean, Wilbur. He's only a baby!'

Winnie stroked her new kitten, tickling behind its ear just as Wilbur liked her to.

PURRRRR! went the kitten.

'I think I'll call you Tights,' said Winnie.

14

But then, 'Oh, my goodness!' said
Winnie, because Tights had just jumped
up onto the table and was eating Winnie's
lunch. Then he jumped down and nudged
open the larder door, and then the fridge
door, and he ate *everything* there . . .

before he jumped onto the draining board,
turned on the tap with his paw, and drank
all the water in the tap. Then he gave
Winnie a look that suggested he was *still*
hungry!

'Er, I think he's still hungry!' said
Winnie. 'I'd better . . .' Winnie took out
her wand. She began to wave it, then—
CRASH! —Tights pounced on the wand.

'That's nice!' said Winnie rather
nervously. 'He wants to play!' She found a
fluffy slipper with long ribbons and tied it
to the end of her wand. Then she dangled
it like a fishing rod, twitching the fluffy
slipper in front of Tights.

Tights stalked the slipper. He was

growling. He was prowling. He was preparing to pounce . . .

'Er, Wilbur?' said Winnie. Her hand was suddenly shaking with fear, making the fluffy slipper twitch even more enticingly. 'Wilbur!'

Wilbur was speedily turning the pages of a *Big Book of Animals*, and when he got to the 'T' page he held it up to show Winnie . . .

'A *tiger*?' said Winnie. 'You mean,
Tights is a t-t-t-t-tiger!'

Pounce! Chomp!

'Wilbuurrr!'

Tights had chomped not just the slipper
and the ribbon, but half of Winnie's wand.

Wilbur beckoned Winnie towards the empty larder.

'Meeow!' he yowled.

Winnie ran inside, and Wilbur slammed the door shut.

Pounce! went Tights.

But Wilbur was too fast for Tights the tiger.

Wilbur clattered out through the cat flap, leaving Winnie trapped in the larder with Tights prowling and growling in the kitchen, and occasionally pushing— **thud!**—at the door or—**clatter!**—at the cat flap that was too small for a tiger to get through.

'Ooer,' wobbled Winnie, watching the larder door. All she could do was wait, sitting on a shelf as if she was food.

21

But—*meeeoow!*—Wilbur was
swinging Tarzan-like on a vine over the
garden wall and in through a window to
Jerry's house.

'Meeow!' he announced to Jerry and
Scruff, and he quickly mimed the story of
what had happened to poor Winnie.

'Wot? Missus needs me?' said

Jerry, and he, Wilbur, and Scruff ran over to Winnie's.

With one giant kick—**BASH!**—he kicked down Winnie's door, and he scooped up Tights the tiger . . . who suddenly looked properly kitten-sized and just a bit scared himself in Jerry's great big hands.

Wilbur opened the larder door, and out wobbled Winnie.

'Ooh, thank you, Wilbur and Jerry and Scruff!' she said. 'Er, I think we might need to take Tights to the zoo.'

So they all trooped along the road to the zoo . . . where the zoo keeper was so happy to receive the tiger that he gave them a reward.

'You can all have free rides,' he said. 'I'll just pop our little tiger into the big wild tiger enclosure.'

'He needs lots to eat,' said Winnie.

Then Jerry rode an elephant, Wilbur and Scruff rode in baskets either side of a zebra, and Winnie rode a camel.

'Just one more thing!' said Winnie, and she waved her wand, *Abracadabra!* And instantly they all had magnificently large ice creams.

'This treat is thanks to you, Wilbur,' said Winnie. 'So you *do* make things fun after all!'

Winnie and Wilbur were so tired when they got home, and so full of ice cream, and there wasn't any food left in the house anyway, that they went straight to bed.

Just as Winnie's eyes closed she said, 'When you were a kitten, Wilbur, you wanted to play . . . even at bedtime.'

Yawn! 'Actually-pactually I'm very glad that you're a boring old cat just now.'

Purrr! went Wilbur.

WINNIE
Goes Camping

The sky was bluebottle blue with just a few little white maggoty clouds. The sun felt as warm as an over-ripe compost heap.

'It's a perfect day for being outside,' sighed Winnie as she pegged out her washing. 'Just smell those pretty ponghorns, Wilbur.'

Sniff went Wilbur. Then his eyes bulged, he stepped back onto a corner of the sheet that Winnie was draping over the clothes line, and—**ah-ah-atishooo!**

—he sneezed a breeze that lifted the other side of the sheet up so that it was caught by a branch. And suddenly Winnie was under a sheet tent.

'Wilbur, you're as clever as a clog-dancing dinosaur!' she said. 'Let's go camping!'

Winnie waved her wand.
'Abracadabra!'

Instantly there was a huge backpack for
Winnie and a small one for Wilbur.

Wilbur packed his comfy blanket, his
whisker cream, and a packet of fishy-bics.
He put on his walking boots.

Winnie packed a tent and a sleeping
bag and hats and coats and gloves. She
packed tins and bottles and bags and boxes
and nets of food. She packed a stove and
matches and cauldrons and spatulas and
graters and squashers and squishers and
plates and knives and forks and spoons and
saucers and a sink . . .

'Meow?' said Wilbur.

'All right, I'll leave the sink,' agreed
Winnie. Then she put on her walking
boots, and then she and Wilbur heaved
and huffed and puffed to get her backpack
onto her back. And off they set towards
the mountains.

They started off very slowly and
Winnie's legs buckled with every step.

But the further they walked, the easier
Winnie found it to carry her big backpack.

Even when they were going up the
mountain and it was getting steep, Winnie
found it easier and easier.

'Ooh, I'm getting *so* fit with all this
fresh air and exercise!' said Winnie.

'What did you say, Wilbur?'

But Wilbur, puffing along beside
Winnie, shook his head. He hadn't said
anything.

'This walking is making me as hungry as
an empty snail shell,' said Winnie. 'When
we get to the top I'll cook us up a cauldron
of slug and gherkin stew with fluffy
fungus dumplings . . . ooh, my mouth's
watering already!'

They went up into the clouds, and at the
very top of the mountain they stopped.
That was when Winnie and Wilbur took
off their backpacks, and Winnie saw . . .

'Oh, dimpled dung beetle bottoms!
There's a blooming hole in my bag, and
everything's fallen out of it!'

36

'Beeeeh,' said a goat, making Winnie jump.

'Where the diddle-daddle did that goat come from?' said Winnie. 'Look! It's scoffing just about everything!'

'Mrrow!' Wilbur held out a paw.

Splat!—a big raindrop fell onto it.

'Have we still got the tent?' said Winnie.

Luckily the tent was one of the last things to fall out of her backpack.

Unluckily the goat had already found
it—**chomp, chomp!**

Winnie and Wilbur fought the wind, the
rain, and the goat to get the tent put up.

'Ooh, I'm as cold as a penguin's toes,'
said Winnie, shivering.

'Where are those fishy-bics of yours,
Wilbur?'

Wilbur handed one little fishy-bic to
Winnie. Winnie looked at it.

'Is that all? I carried far more than you
did up this mountain, you know!'

'Meow,' said Wilbur, who was of course
right that Winnie was also the one to have
lost the most stuff up the mountain.

'You've got to share!' said Winnie,
snatching the fishy-bic packet from Wilbur.
'I will share them fairly.' And Winnie began
making two piles of little biscuits. 'One for
me, one for you, one for me, one for you,
one for . . . Oh, there's one left over. And
it's the turn for "one for me", so . . .'

'Mrrow!' Wilbur snatched the biscuit
from her. After all, he was the one who had
brought them.

40

'But I'm bigger, so I need more food!'
said Winnie. **Snatch!**

'Meeow!' Wilbur was about to snatch
again when Winnie held up a hand. 'Let's
have a competition. The winner gets the last
fishy-bic. That's fair.'

'Meeow?'

'Well, we can, er . . .' Winnie looked around the bare wet tent with a grassy floor. 'We'll have a snail race! The one with the winning snail gets the last biscuit. Here's the start, and here's the finish. OK?' Wilbur nodded.

So they chose a snail each, and put them at the start.

'Are you ready, are you steady?' said Winnie. 'Get set, go!' And the snails began to move ever so . . . ever so . . . ever so slowly. **Yawn.**

'Mine's a tentacle in the lead!' said Winnie at last. But neither snail was getting anywhere near the finishing line.

'Oh, I'm *so* hungry!' wailed Winnie.
Then she sat up. 'But I've just had a
brillaramaroodles idea! Why don't we
break the last fishy-bic in half, and have
half each?'

'Meeow!' agreed Wilbur.

They were just reaching out to eat
the fishy-bics at last when—**chomp!**
chomp!—the goat stuck its head through
a hole in the tent, and ate the lot.

Gulp! went Winnie and Wilbur. They looked at the empty place where the fishy-bics had been ... and saw the snails sliding over to slobber up the very last little crumb.

'Shall we go home?' said Winnie.

45

It was easy to find their way back down
the mountain because they could follow
the trail of the dropped things that even
a goat couldn't eat. The rain had stopped,
and everything was eerily beautiful in the
moonlight.

46

'Pass me that stove, Wilbur,' said
Winnie. 'We might be cold and aching and
starving hungry, but we're not going to
leave litter to spoil the mountain.'

The goat had followed them with a
rather pleased look on its face. When they
got halfway down the mountain Winnie
suddenly said, 'Uh-oh! There's another
blooming goat!'

48

But this one wasn't a goat, in spite of the
beard. It was a farmer who was so glad to
have his goat back that he gave Winnie
and Wilbur a loaf of bread and a soft
squidgy goat's cheese.

So, when they got home, Winnie made cheese sandwiches. They had one sandwich each but there was one left over. 'You have the extra one, Wilbur,' said Winnie, who was feeling as if she'd had enough of anything to do with goats for one day.

'Meeow,' said Wilbur, pushing the plate
back towards Winnie.

'I don't want it! It's yours!' said Winnie...

And they quarrelled until they fell asleep
at the table.

WINNIE'S

Hat Trick

One bright sunny lunchtime Winnie and Wilbur flew over the school where the little ordinaries were playing outside.

Winnie shouted down to the children, 'Wilbur and I are going to the fair!'

'We have to stay at school, and that's *not* fair!' shouted back the little ordinaries.

'Oh deary lumpy-dumplings,' said Winnie. 'Poor little ordinaries.' But she soon forgot about them as she and Wilbur flew above the fair.

'Wowsy, Wilbur, listen to that music! Smell the oniony-buniony smells! Ooh, just listen to those big squeals coming from the big wheel! Shall we have a ride on that before anything else?'

'Meow!' agreed Wilbur, his whiskers twirling with excitement as Winnie steered her broom down to land in the fairground.

They scoffed pink candy floss off sticks as they headed towards the higher-than-a-house big wheel.

But when they got there, a girl said, 'You can't go on the big wheel.' She pointed at Winnie. 'You're too tall.' Then she pointed at Wilbur. 'You're too small. See?' She pointed at a height chart. She was right.

'Oh, we can sort that problem, easy-
peasy elephant-with-a-bad-cold-sneezy!'
said Winnie. She took off her hat, and put
it onto Wilbur's head. 'See? Now he's tall
enough and I'm short enough. All right all
left?' And she climbed into one of the seats
and put down the bar.

'Meeow?' asked Wilbur a little
nervously because he really was rather
small for the seat.

56

'Don't be a scaredy cat, Wilbur,' said Winnie. '*Weee*, here we go!'

The wheel turned, and Winnie and Wilbur's seat lurched backwards and swung a bit as it went up ... up ...

'Mrrow!'

Wilbur's eyes were suddenly covered
by Winnie's hat sliding over them so that
he couldn't see anything. The lurching
backwards was starting to make him feel a
bit sick.

'MEEOW!' wailed Wilbur, and he
knocked the hat right off his head, just
as their seat swung to the very top of the
wheel . . . and then started going down . . .
down . . . down, forwards.

'My hat!' wailed Winnie, watching
it falling through the air and whoopsy-
wafting on the breeze. 'My hat's going to
land on the ghost train!'

59

Winnie and Wilbur jumped off the big wheel seat as soon as it got to the ground. Wilbur's legs were woozily wobbly with fright, but Winnie held his paw, and they ran to the ghost train.

'It's already moving! Quick, Wilbur!'

Leap! They jumped onto the last carriage of the train, just as Winnie's

hat on the front carriage disappeared
into a tunnel. **Whoo! Shriek!** went
the ghosties and witches in the tunnel,
looming out of the darkness.

'Boo to you!' shouted Winnie. 'I'm a
witch too!'

Eeek! They all ran away. But Winnie's
hat was still out of reach.

It was out of the tunnel before Winnie
and Wilbur were, and a man snatched it up
and ran off with it, putting it on his head
to make his girlfriend laugh.

'Oi, it's not funny! It's a serious hat!
Give it back!' shouted Winnie. And she
chased the man, with Wilbur chasing
her, and a baby girl chasing Wilbur's

tail, and the baby girl's mum chasing the
baby girl. They all followed Winnie's
hat—**wheee!**—down the helter-skelter,
around and around in the spinning
teacups, up—**boing!**—on the reverse
bungee, and all over—**bump!**—the
dodgems floor as the evening grew dark
and the stars came out.

'It's no good, Wilbur. We've had lots of goes on lots of rides, but I've lost my hat forever and I'll never get it back now,' said Winnie sadly.

Winnie thought about hats as she and Wilbur flew home. She thought about hats all night.

In the morning Winnie picked up her
wand and waved it,

Abracadabra!'

Instantly there was a beautiful helter-
skelter hat.

'Whirly and nice, and almost like my
old one!' said Winnie. 'Hmm. But perhaps
it's time for a change to a different kind of
hat?' So, *'Abracadabra!'*

Winnie magicked a candy floss hat.

'*Abracadabra!*' A carousel hat.

'*Abracadabra!*' And—**zap! zap! zap!**—

there were hats flying everywhere!

'Meeow?' said Wilbur.

'Good question, hat cat!' said Winnie.

'What am I going to do with them all? Ooh!' Winnie's eyes gleamed. 'I've just had a brillaramaroodles idea! Hand me my mobile moan, Wilbur. I'm going to ring Mrs Parmar at the school.'

ALERT!
WINNIE
the
WITCH
CALLING
WARNING
13131313

67

Wilbur made a big poster that said:

Mrs Parmar brought all the children out
of school and into Winnie's garden.

There was a silly hat for each of them,

even one for Mrs Parmar. And there were
lots of hats left over for playing hat games.

There was the hat slalom.

There was a hat shy.

There were hat relay races.

There was a best-garden-in-a-hat

contest.

Winnie ran the stall for playing guess
which hat the frog is under.

Jerry had a giant chip stall, serving hats
full of chips.

Wilbur and Scruff did a magic act,
pulling rabbits out of hats.

As the children left at the end of the day, Winnie told Wilbur, 'I think that I like silly hat days even better than I like fairs.'

'Meeow,' agreed Wilbur.

'But, silly-slug-sausage-me, I've gone and given away *all* the hats I made, so now I *still* haven't got one for myself!' said Winnie. 'Which one of them all do you think I would look prettiest in, Wilbur?'

71

Wilbur scratched a claw in the earth to draw a hat . . . exactly like the hats that Winnie had always worn before. Winnie laughed.

'You're as right as a left boot on a left foot, Wilbur!' said Winnie. 'I liked my dear old hat the best of them all, too.'

So she waved her wand. '*Abracadabra!*'
And there was a hat just like the ones she
had before. It was comfortable. It was just
the right hat for Winnie.

'Ahhh!' sighed Winnie happily.
'*Abracadabra!*' And she made a little one,
almost the same, for Wilbur . . . but his hat
had ear holes in it.

73

ΣΑΜΣΟΥΝΓ 100

74

WINNIE
the Bold

Crackle! Clunk! Blaaank!

'Oh no!' Winnie jumped up as if an alligator had bitten her bottom, sending Wilbur flying through the air.

'Mrrow!'

'The blooming telly's gone off!' Winnie pushed buttons on her remote control. 'That film was as exciting as opening a present that's the shape of a dinosaur on a bike. And now we're missing it, Wilbur!'

Wilbur yawned wide.

'Didn't you see those little ordinaries in the film? They went into a wardrobe and they came out into a different land! There were witches and lions, just like you and me, really, Wilbur, so . . .' Winnie's eyes went dreamy. 'Ooh, Wilbur, shall we go and have our own adventure? Right now?'

Suddenly Wilbur was wide awake, shaking his head and backing away from

Winnie, but—**snatch!**—Winnie grabbed him.

'Come on, Wilbur. We need a wardrobe! There's one in my bedroom.'

'Mrrow!' protested Wilbur, but Winnie marched up the stairs, opened the wardrobe, and—**swish-swoosh**—pushed through her clothes to . . .

'Wowsy!' said Winnie. Then, 'Yikes in tights, there's a tin man on a horse coming straight at us!' Winnie jumped to one side, just as a knight on a sleek black horse galloped past. And another man was talking to Winnie.

'Your turn in the joust, Sire. Here is your steed.' He held out reins attached to a huge cloppety white horse. 'Your squire will help you to mount your steed.'

78

'My *what* will help me to *what* my *what*?' said Winnie.

Wilbur was holding his paws as a step for Winnie, so she climbed up and onto the horse.

'Meeow!' suggested Wilbur, jumping up behind her.

'Good thinking!' said Winnie, and she waved her wand. *'Abracadabra!'*

Instantly she and Wilbur were dressed
in armour. 'Oooer, this is a bit stiff!' said
Winnie. She held on tight. Wilbur did too,
with claws.

Neeiiiggh! Up reared the horse, and
then off it galloped—**thuddery-thud!**—
with Winnie and Wilbur clinging on.

80

'That tin man's coming for us again!'
shouted Winnie. 'And he's pointing a big
stick at us. That's as rude as a bare bear's
bottom, that is!'

Winnie held her wand out, but it
suddenly looked very small. So,
    Abracadabra!

Instantly the wand was big and long,
and—**CRASH!**—it hit the other knight's
lance.

'He's blooming well bent my wand!' wailed Winnie. She waved it. '*Abracadabra!*'

Winnie turned her horse, and so did the other knight. They charged towards each other again, but this time Winnie's wand was sparking and smoking and— **kerboom!**—it made a noise that made the sleek black horse and its rider turn and flee.

'Hooray!' cheered a huge crowd of people that Winnie hadn't even noticed before. Trumpets parped as Winnie and Wilbur—**crash, crumple!**—got down off their horse.

They were carried as heroes to the king's banqueting table.

'Eat and drink and make merry!' declared the king from his throne. 'Then you, bold knight, must go and rescue my daughter!'

'Um.' **Munch!** 'Rescue her from what, your kinginess?' asked Winnie, trying to post food through her helmet as if it was a letter box.

'From the dragon!' said the king.

Cough! Out came the food that
Winnie had posted. *'Dragon!'* said Winnie.

Wilbur tried to slide-hide under the
table.

'Yes, the dragon lives in the cave up
there.' The king pointed. 'Off you go.'

So Winnie and Wilbur did go. **Clank-clank-clank.** The nearer they got to the cave, the more slowly they went.

'This is as scary as a hairy-chested fairy!' said Winnie. 'But we must save that poor 'iccle princess who . . . '

'Leave me alone!' cried a voice from inside the cave.

86

'Come on, Wilbur!' Winnie—**clank-clank**—ran into the cave. 'Ooh, it's as dark as . . . oh!' A sudden flare of light showed the princess struggling with something.

'Let her go, you bully!' shouted Winnie, whacking her wand at where she thought the dragon must be.

'Ouch! Not you as well!' sighed the
voice that they'd heard earlier, and it
wasn't coming from the princess.

'Er ... *Abracadabra!*' went Winnie,
so that her wand lit up the whole cave.
Then, 'Oh!' said Winnie. The dragon
was not much bigger than Wilbur. It was
holding onto a rock as the princess tugged
at its tail.

'I want a dragon pet but this one's being naughty and won't come with me!' The princess took a very deep breath, and, 'Waaah!' she wailed.

Wilbur clamped a paw over her mouth.

'This isn't how it works in books and films!' said Winnie. **Clank-screech!** Winnie bent down in her armour. 'Little dragon, you seem sensible, so could you tell us what's going on here?'

'I was in my cave minding my own business when *she* came along!' The little dragon pointed at the princess. 'And she tried to dragon-nap me!'

'**Mmmnbbfff,**' said the Princess.

'You can take your paw off her mouth now, Wilbur,' said Winnie.

'I wanted adventure!' said the princess. 'I thought dragon-hunting would be exciting . . . but all I found was this useless creature!'

'Tell you what,' suggested Winnie, 'do you want to have a go at being a knight? I'll swap if you like! Then you can have fun poking people with sticks, and Wilbur and I can go back to the castle and find a wardrobe to get us home again.'

'Do you think that I might come with you?' asked the little dragon. 'I don't like the idea of the princess with a big stick being *anywhere* near me!'

'Why not,' said Winnie. She waved her wand. *Abracadabra!*' And instantly Winnie looked like a princess, the princess looked like a knight, and Wilbur and the dragon looked like themselves.

'Right. Where will I find the best wardrobe in the castle?' asked Winnie.

'In Daddy's— I mean the king's— dressing room,' said the princess knight.

It was a good wardrobe. Winnie, Wilbur, and the dragon sank straight through the soft, mothball-smelly cloaks to arrive back at . . .

'Home, sweet stinky-feet home!' said
Winnie, pulling off the princess dress that
itched.

They toasted marsh-smellows on sticks
in the little dragon's breath, and dipped
them into sugared frogspawn.

'Ah, a feast fit for a king!' said Winnie.

'Meeow!'

'Or for witches and cats and dragons!'

'I would very much like a cave of my own,' yawned the little dragon.

'Well, if you fly into those woods out there, I'm sure you'll find a lovely cave with no princesses to annoy you,' said Winnie.

She and Wilbur waved the dragon goodbye. Then they went to bed.

Good knight, Winnie the Bold!

Enjoy more magic moments with
Winnie and Wilbur

KORKY